Anyone Can Eat Squid!

by **Phyllis Reynolds Naylor**

illustrated by **Marcy Ramsey**

Marshall Cavendish Children

To Paige Saah
—*P. R. N.*

Text copyright © 2005 by Phyllis Reynolds Naylor
Illustrations copyright © 2005 by Marshall Cavendish
First Marshall Cavendish paperback edition, 2009

Marshall Cavendish, 99 White Plains Road, Tarrytown, NY 10591
www.marshallcavendish.us/kids

Library of Congress Cataloging-in-Publication Data
Naylor, Phyllis Reynolds
Anyone can eat squid! / by Phyllis Reynolds Naylor ; illustrated by Marcy Ramsey.—
1st ed.
p. cm. — (Simply Sarah)
Summary: Sarah longs to find a way to be someone special, and when her friend's
Chinese restaurant needs customers, she finds a special way to save it.
978-0-7614-5182-2 (hardcover) 978-0-7614-5540-0 (paperback)
[1. Advertising—Fiction. 2. Individuality—Fiction.] I. Ramsey, Marcy Dunn, ill. II. Title.
III. Series.
PZ7.N24An 2005
[Fic]—dc22
2004021132

The illustrations are rendered in ink and wash.

Printed in China
A Marshall Cavendish Chapter Book

2 4 6 5 3 1

Contents

One

Meet Sarah

What Sarah Simpson wanted more than anything in the world was to be special somehow. She wanted to look different or feel different or do something that was extra-ordinary.

Maybe she could pick one thing and get very good at it, she thought. Jumping rope or doing math problems. Drawing pictures or chasing chickens. What would it be?

Jumping rope wouldn't do, however. At recess, each girl took a turn at jumping while the others chanted a silly verse. They made the verses embarrassing so the girl who was jumping would miss. When Sarah began to jump, they sang out:

Sarah Simpson
sitting in a tree,
p-o-o-p-i-n-g!

And Sarah tripped over the rope.

Being extra good at math problems wasn't the answer, either: *If Mr. Brown sells nine cans of tomatoes a day, how many will he sell in a week? A year?* Sarah didn't care about Mr. Brown and his tomatoes. She didn't even like tomatoes.

When she tried to draw a picture of her family—Sarah; her mom; her brother, Riley; and her dad, who worked overseas building bridges—her people looked like dead bugs. They didn't look anything at all like the pictures her mom painted.

As for chickens, it was Sarah's job to keep them out of the newly planted vegetable garden when she went to visit Grandpa.

Sarah had thought she was very good at flapping her arms like a big chicken and chasing the hens back to the chicken yard where they belonged. Except that the old rooster decided to chase Sarah. He pecked at the backs of her legs until she ran up on the porch. No, she wasn't good at chasing chickens, either.

But four-year-old Riley thought his sister was special. When Sarah fixed the wheel on his truck, he said, "Sarah can do anything!"

Right! thought Sarah. *Anyone can fix a wheel on a toy truck.*

Sarah's mom thought her daughter was special. When Sarah made a salad of carrots and apples and raisins, her mom said, "Why, it's wonderful, Sarah! You're a great little cook!"

Sure, thought Sarah. *Anyone can scrape a carrot*.

Sarah's grandpa thought she was special, too.

"You can grow up to be anything you want, even president," he told her once.

Not! Sarah said to herself.

Her dad sent her funny letters addressed to *The Very Best Daughter in the Whole World*. But Sarah knew that as much as her family loved her, she was just plain ordinary. The most unusual thing she had ever done was bite the dentist's fingers. Even her name was ordinary.

Sarah sat down on the stairs outside her apartment and tried to figure out a way to be special. But an hour went by, and afternoon became evening. Sarah could hear the clatter of pans and knew that her mom had put her painting away and started dinner. She heard the TV come on and knew that Riley was watching cartoons.

Sarah sighed and leaned against the railing. She had plain brown hair, not red like Riley's. She had plain gray eyes, not green like her mom's. She had short stubby fingers, not long like her dad's.

Even her skin was ordinary, not the color of cocoa like her friend Peter's, who lived in the apartment below. And she couldn't count in Chinese, like Tim at school.

If there was anything special about her, she decided, it was that she was the most ordinary girl in the apartment building. The most ordinary girl on the block. The most ordinary girl in Chicago and the whole United States. And that just wasn't extraordinary enough for Sarah Simpson.

Two

Pork Chops, Peas, and Potatoes

Sarah stared down at her plate, at the potato and pork chop and spoonful of green peas. She speared the pork chop with her fork and held it in front of her face, turning it slowly around and around.

"Is there a problem?" asked Mom.

Sarah sighed. "A plain old girl eating a plain old pork chop," she said wistfully.

"I don't see anything wrong with that," said Mom.

Sarah sighed again, a longer, louder sigh. "Why don't we ever eat snails, like they do in France?"

7

"*Snails?*" said Mom.

Riley stopped chewing and stared at his sister. "You can eat worms!" he said.

"I just want to eat something *different!*" Sarah said. "I'm tired of potatoes. I'm tired of doing the same old thing all the time. I'm tired of being the same old me."

"You could go to school with a paper bag over your head," Mom teased.

Sarah scowled. "I want to *be* something special. I want people to look at me and say, 'Here comes Sarah Simpson!'"

Riley looked at her. "Here comes Sarah Simpson!" he said.

"Not you," said Sarah. "I'm just so ordinary, Mom! I'm not best at anything."

"Usually people who are best at something do it because they like to. They don't worry too much about being special," Mom said.

"But you're special at painting!" Sarah told her. "You're the best artist in Chicago, aren't you?"

"Not by a long shot," Mom said.

8

"You're the best artist on our block, I'll bet!" said Sarah.

"I doubt it," said Mom.

"You're the best artist in our building, then," said Sarah.

"I don't know everyone in our building," said Mom. "But I'll tell you what. I'm a little tired of potatoes and pork chops, too, so we'll go out to dinner on Saturday. Where would you like to go?"

"Wongs'!" cried Sarah and Riley together.

"For chicken wings!" said Riley, smacking his lips.

"Then that's just what we'll do," said Mom.

The next morning Sarah left for school. As usual, she stopped at the apartment below to walk with Peter Grant.

Peter's grandmother opened the door. Granny Belle always had slippers on her feet, a sweater around her shoulders, and a smile on her face.

"Is Peter ready?" asked Sarah.

"As ready as he'll ever be," said Granny Belle. She called to Peter. "Wipe the toothpaste off your mouth, Peter, and get your backpack. Sarah's here."

Peter came to the door. Granny Belle took his face in her hands and kissed him on both cheeks. Peter tried to get away, but she pulled him back and kissed him on the forehead.

Sarah and Peter ran down the stairs toward the second floor. As Peter raised one hand to his face, his grandmother called after him: "And don't you wipe off that kiss, young man. *That* one's for good luck!"

Sarah and Peter laughed and went on down to the first floor.

Outside, the air was sweet and smelled of spring. Peter's legs were long, and he always seemed to be a step or two ahead of Sarah. His backpack looked like all the other backpacks at school. His clothes were the ordinary kind. Just like hers, his name was ordinary, Sarah was thinking.

"If you could change one thing about yourself, what would it be?" Sarah asked him.

"Nothing," said Peter.

"Not even your name?" Sarah asked.

"No. I like it fine," said Peter.

Some people didn't mind being ordinary!

When Sarah walked into the classroom, Mrs. Gold wasn't there. A new teacher was standing at the front of the room. Sarah heard her tell some boys that Mrs. Gold was sick.

And suddenly an idea popped into Sarah's head. She looked around for Emily Watson, who was getting her workbook off the shelf.

Sarah went over and whispered, "Just for today, you be Sarah Simpson, and I'll be Emily Watson. Okay?"

Emily's eyes grew as big as Ping-Pong balls, and then she began to smile. "Okay," she said.

Three

Trading Names

Sarah could hardly keep from laughing. What a great idea! For at least *one* day she could be someone different. The new teacher wrote her name on the blackboard so everyone would know who she was: Miss Bowers.

Sarah took Emily's workbook, and Emily took hers. But when Sarah sat at Emily's desk and Emily sat at hers, the other kids opened their mouths wide in surprise and pointed. Sarah grinned and put her finger to her lips to let them in on the joke.

13

Miss Bowers took the roll. "Please raise your hand when I call your name," she said. She started with "Justin Adams," then "David Bork." When she got to "Sarah Simpson," Emily raised her hand and said, "Here!"

A few giggles went around the room. The teacher looked up. The giggles stopped. When she got to "Emily Watson," Sarah raised *her* hand and said, "Here!"

Again Sarah heard some giggles.

Miss Bowers looked around the class. "What's funny?" she asked. The smiles disappeared. "Then let's get out our readers," the teacher said.

There weren't enough of the new reading books to go around, so everyone had to share.

"Here, Emily, you can be my partner," one of the girls said to Sarah, with a smile.

"Hey, Sarah, you can share my book," David Bork said to Emily. He was smiling, too.

When Sarah's reading group had taken its place in the circle, Miss Bowers looked at her list of names and called on different people to read.

"Emily, would you read the next page, please?" she asked after a while.

The real Emily opened her mouth to begin, but Sarah caught it in time: "*The prince called for his horse, and off he went*," she read. She peeped at Emily over the page, and they grinned at each other.

This is fun! Sarah decided. She liked being Emily Watson for a day. No one else in the class had ever done this before. When they took their spelling test, the real Sarah Simpson got all her words right, and the real Emily Watson missed four.

Miss Bowers asked how many had spelled all the words correctly, and Sarah and Peter held up their hands. The teacher wrote *Peter Grant* and *Emily Watson* on the blackboard and put stars by their names in yellow chalk. Then she collected the papers to write the scores in the teacher's grade book.

Sarah swallowed. The real Sarah Simpson was going to get a minus four, and the real Emily Watson was going to get a star!

At recess, everyone was talking about how Sarah and Emily had changed places.

"You're going to get in big trouble, I'll bet," said Peter, bouncing a basketball around and around on the cement.

"It's only for a day," said Sarah.

"What if Mrs. Gold is sick for a month? What if you have to keep on being Emily till she gets back?" he said.

The little seed of worry in Sarah's head began to grow. But when it was time for lunch and nothing bad had happened, Sarah forgot about being worried. She and Emily traded lunches. Emily ate Sarah's egg-salad sandwich, and Sarah ate Emily's turkey and cheese.

When Tim Wong passed by Sarah's table, she said, "Hey, Tim, we're going to eat at your restaurant on Saturday."

17

"That's good," he said.

That afternoon, Miss Bowers started talking about a new unit in geography. Sarah wasn't paying attention. She and Tim were watching a bug crawl along a boy's shirt collar. The boy didn't know it was there. Sarah giggled.

"Emily, please," the teacher said, but Sarah went on giggling.

"Emily?" Miss Bowers said again.

Someone poked Sarah.

"Sarah!" somebody whispered.

Sarah sat up stiffly and looked around.

Miss Bowers continued: "We're going to be studying Alaska, our forty-ninth state. There are three questions on the blackboard, and every day there will be new ones for us to think about. Above those questions, I would like someone to write *Alaska* in big fancy letters with colored chalk. Who would like to do that?"

At least half the class had their hands in the air. Sarah stretched her arm up as high as it would go and waved it madly around in circles. She liked to make letters with colored chalk. She would make the letter A extra fancy using blue and white to remind people of icebergs and snow.

"Sarah, how about you?" Miss Bowers said, checking her seating chart.

Sarah rose up out of her chair, and so did Emily. They stared at each other, and Miss Bowers stared at them.

And then the teacher said, "Will the real Sarah Simpson please come to the front of the room?"

Emily sat back down. Sarah could feel her cheeks growing hot. Her ears were hot. Her neck was hot. She walked slowly up the aisle toward the teacher.

"Are you sitting at Emily's desk?" Miss Bowers asked.

Sarah nodded.

"Were you using Emily's workbook?" Miss Bowers asked.

Sarah nodded again.

"Why?" the teacher asked.

"Because I wanted to be somebody different," Sarah said in a teeny tiny voice.

Everyone laughed. Even Peter. Even *Emily*!

Miss Bowers smiled a little. "Well, since you are the only person you can ever be, would the real Sarah Simpson like to write *Alaska* on the blackboard in big fancy letters?"

Sarah took the chalk and began.

Four

Broom

"See? I didn't get in trouble!" Sarah told Peter on the way home.

"How do you know?" said Peter. "Maybe she didn't change your spelling grade in the teacher's book."

Sometimes Peter got on Sarah's nerves. He had been her friend for a whole year, ever since he and his grandmother had moved into the apartment building. But she hadn't wanted to think about that spelling grade.

"So?" she said. "Didn't *you* ever do anything wrong at school?"

"Sure," said Peter.

"What was the worst thing you ever did?" Sarah asked.

"I killed something."

Sarah stopped walking and stared at him. "*What*?"

"Our hamster. The teacher wanted someone to take it home over spring vacation, but I didn't think Granny Belle would like the idea, so I hid it in my room."

"What happened?"

"I let it run around all over my bed. Then Granny Belle called me to come turn off the TV. I guess I didn't close the door all the way behind me, and the hamster got out. It ran across Granny Belle's foot in the kitchen. She thought it was a rat and killed it with a broom."

"That's terrible!" Sarah said. "But *you* didn't kill it."

"I sure felt like I had," said Peter. "When Granny Belle found out it was a hamster, she said that keeping it secret was like telling a lie.

And any boy who would lie to his grandmother would do almost any awful abomination that came to mind."

"Any awful *what*?" said Sarah.

"That's what Granny called it," said Peter. "It means any awful thing."

Sarah couldn't imagine her friend Peter doing anything too awful. "Then what?" she asked. "How did you tell your teacher?"

"Granny Belle laid the hamster's body in a shoe box and stuck it in the freezer. When vacation was over, she put on her hat and her Sunday dress and marched me to school, carrying the frozen hamster."

Now Sarah could imagine it very well.

"I had to hand the box to the teacher and tell the whole class what had happened, while Granny Belle stood in the doorway like this." Peter crossed his arms in front of him and stuck out his lower lip. "I had to say that I would take all the money I had saved to go to a basketball game and buy another hamster for the class."

"Did you?" asked Sarah.

"Yeah. The class named it Broom."

This time Sarah laughed, and so did Peter.

When they reached their apartment building, Sarah said, "Mom's doing pictures for a book about a hamster. You want to see them?"

"Sure," said Peter.

They went up the first flight of stairs to the second floor. They went up the second flight of stairs to the third, and finally the last flight of stairs to the fourth.

Sarah's family had the whole top floor. It was two apartments put together, and it didn't have any walls dividing the space into rooms. It was called a loft. Sarah's mother used bookcases and screens for walls.

There was a skylight at one end of the loft, and Mom did her painting under the skylight. She painted pictures to hang on people's walls. She drew pictures to go in children's books. She painted signs to go over doorways and posters to go in shop windows.

Sometimes, when Sarah opened the door to their apartment, she smelled banana bread, and sometimes she smelled paint. Today it was paint.

Riley ran to the door to meet them and held out both fists. "Look!" he said. Mom had painted a hamster's face on the back of each hand—a funny-looking hamster with big teeth.

Sarah closed the door behind them. "Peter's here," she called.

"Come on in, Peter," Mom called back.

Sarah led him past the couch and chairs, the rug and bookcases, the window and the two beds where she and Riley slept, until they reached the end of the loft beneath the skylight.

It was messy there. Drops of paint were splattered across the wood floor. Finished pictures were propped up on tables, and half-finished sketches were taped to the brick walls. There were books and brushes and paints and chalk and color everywhere. *Walking into Mom's studio is like walking into a rainbow,* Sarah thought.

"Peter wants to see the pictures you're doing for that book about a hamster," she said. She decided she wouldn't tell the story about a hamster named Broom. Not in front of Riley, anyway.

"I've been working on them all week," Mom said. She was wearing a large shirt with paint stains on the front and the sleeves. She had pinned her hair up high on her head so as not to get paint in it. She pointed to the drawings on a table.

"I've finished only two of them, but I sort of like this little fellow and his hamster sister," Mom said.

Riley proudly showed off his mother's pictures as though he had drawn them himself. "His name's Whiskers," he said, pointing to the hamster in the blue pants and the red baseball cap.

27

"What happens in the story?" Sarah asked.

"The hamster buys a cap that's way too big for him, but it's the only red one he can find. And he gets in a lot of trouble because the cap keeps slipping down over his eyes and he can't see. So he gives the cap to his daddy for his birthday," Mom explained.

"Did you write the story?" Peter asked Sarah's mother.

"No, I only paint the pictures for other people's stories," she said. She leaned forward with her brush and put a little dab of white on one of the hamster's ears. "How was school?" she asked.

Sarah looked at Peter, and Peter looked at Sarah.

"Okay," said Sarah. "At least it was different."

"There are some peanut-butter cookies in the jar," Mom said. "Help yourselves."

"Me too!" said Riley, running back to the middle of the loft where the stove and refrigerator stood.

Sarah got down some glasses and poured the milk. She put the big jar in the middle of the table, and they each took a couple of cookies. Peter had just taken a bite when there was a loud knock at the door. Sarah went to answer.

There stood Granny Belle looking as mad as a hornet.

Five

Granny Belle Gets Mad

"Peter Jefferson Grant!" Granny Belle thundered.

Riley jumped.

Peter got up from the table and stood as straight as a soldier, a cookie still in his mouth.

"What do you mean by coming up here and not even telling your granny you're home?" the old lady scolded, yanking him by the arm. "How did I know you weren't run over by a truck? How did I know you hadn't broken both legs and your neck besides? If you can't be a help, boy, don't be a tribulation."

She didn't look or sound like the same Granny Belle who had kissed Peter twice that morning and once again for good luck. Sarah didn't know what a tribulation was, but she guessed it was nothing good.

"Sorry," said Peter. "I just came up to see something."

"Looks to me like you came up to *eat* something," said Granny Belle.

"Peanut-butter cookies!" said Riley.

"Is that you, Mrs. Grant?" Mom called from the back of the loft. She came walking toward the front door, wiping her hands on her shirt.

"Yes, it's me, come to fetch my grandson. Like to worry me to death!" said the old woman.

"He was just looking at some pictures I painted for a book. How about a cup of tea and some cookies?" said Mom. "I'm going to have some myself."

Granny Belle was still frowning at Peter, but finally she said, "Well, don't mind if I do."

She sat down on a chair, her feet planted firmly on the floor. Fixing her eyes on her grandson while Mom made the tea, she asked, "What did you learn at school today?"

For a moment it looked to Sarah as though Peter was going to laugh. "I learned not to trade names with anyone," he said.

"Why, I should think not! Peter Jefferson Grant is a perfectly good name," said his grandmother. "What were you thinking of changing it to?"

"Peter Watson, maybe." Peter *was* trying not to laugh, Sarah could tell.

"Watson? What's so special about that?" asked Granny Belle.

"Nothing," said Peter. "Nothing at all."

"Sarah wants to be special," said Riley. "She wants to eat snails."

Granny Belle turned and peered over her glasses at Sarah. "Snails?" she said.

Mom laughed. "Actually, we're thinking of going to Wongs' Restaurant on Saturday night, just for something different. Why don't you and Peter come with us?"

"Yeah! *Can* we, Granny?" Peter asked.

"Not if you're going to eat snails, you're not," said his grandmother.

Mom smiled. "You can both order whatever you like. It's our favorite restaurant."

"Well, I might like some chop suey, if the restaurant's still open," said Granny Belle. "I heard that it might close down."

"Oh, you must be mistaken," said Mom. "Wongs' is a wonderful place to eat. We always go there when we want barbecued chicken wings. Wongs' Wings, they call them."

"Now, that does sound good," said Granny Belle. "Peter and I would love to go with you."

After Peter and his grandmother had gone back down to their apartment, Sarah said, "That can't be true about Wongs' Restaurant closing! I'll ask Tim at school tomorrow."

"Tell him I'll give them all my money if

they keep the restaurant open," said Riley.

Sarah smiled at her little brother. "How much money do you have?" she asked.

"One nickel and one quarter and six pennies," he told her.

As Sarah helped with the dishes that evening, she said, "I didn't know Peter's middle name was Jefferson. Why don't I have a middle name?"

"Because *Sarah Simpson* seemed perfectly lovely to me just the way it is," said Mom. "Simply *Sarah*."

"Well, I wish I had a middle name," Sarah told her. "Something extraordinary."

"What would you like it to be?" asked Mom.

Sarah tried to think of the most unusual names she had ever heard. "Victoria," she said. "Or Celeste. No . . . Octavia. Or maybe Jasmine." There were so many names to choose from.

"You might want to start with an initial and see what works best with *Sarah* and *Simpson*," said Mom. "If you decide you really want a middle name, we could add one someday."

Sarah hadn't known it would be that easy. She began reciting letters of the alphabet in her head, connecting them to her name. *Sarah A. Simpson . . . Sarah B. Simpson . . . Sarah C. Simpson . . . .* She was still thinking of them when she went to sleep that night and decided she liked the letter *T* best of all. *Sarah T. Simpson.* That's who she would be.

Six

Tornadoes and Tacos

Sarah woke early the next morning and thought about wearing something different to go with her new name.

It had to be something no one else had ever worn to school before.

It had to be beautiful.

It had to be something she could wear summer and winter, fall and spring.

It had to be something so different and beautiful that whenever people saw her, they would say, "Here comes Sarah T. Simpson!"

She thought of wearing her red knee-high boots, but those would be too hot in the summer.

She thought of making a gorgeous hat out of paper, but that would blow off in the wind.

Quietly, she got out of bed and went to the big storage closet at one end of the loft. In the Valentine's Day box, she found the pink satin heart with ribbons and roses that Mom hung on their apartment door every February 14. She could wear ribbons in her hair, Sarah thought.

In the Fourth of July box, she found red, white, and blue decorations. She could wear a flag around her shoulders like a cape, Sarah told herself. In the Halloween box, she found vampire fangs and witch's fingernails. She could go to school with her nails painted green.

But in the Christmas box, Sarah found the perfect thing—a long red ribbon with tiny bells sewn on it that Mom hung on the

doorknob of their apartment so that the bells tinkled merrily whenever anyone went in or out.

Sarah chose brown pants and a yellow top to wear to school. Then she took some safety pins from her mother's sewing box and carefully pinned the red ribbon with the bells on it to the bottom of the yellow top.

When she came to breakfast later, Riley said, "I hear Santa Claus!"

Sarah grinned. Now her friends would know she was coming even before she got there! This was her best idea yet!

"You look like you're going to a party," her mother said.

"This is the new me," said Sarah.

On the way to school, Sarah said, "Mom says I can choose a middle name, and I want it to begin with the letter *T*. *Sarah T. Simpson*."

"Tinkerbell," said Peter. "That's what you sound like."

40

"A *real* name," said Sarah.

"Tornado," said Peter.

Sarah wished she hadn't told Peter about her name, because when they got to the playground, he told everyone else. All the kids began suggesting silly names that began with a *T*.

"Turkey!" somebody said.

"Toilet!" said someone else.

"Twinkie," said Tim.

"Tacos!" said Emily. "Sarah Tacos Simpson."

Never tell Peter anything, Sarah said to herself as they went inside. At least she still had her bells.

Mrs. Gold was back. She liked the word *Alaska* that Sarah had drawn on the blackboard with blue and white chalk. Mrs. Gold said the letters looked like icicles.

"You'll find some questions about Alaska on the board," she told the class. "Open your geography books and see if you can find the answers."

41

All the kids opened their books and started to read, while Mrs. Gold checked her grade book.

Sarah remembered trading names with Emily. What if Miss Bowers hadn't changed the spelling grade beside her name? What if there was still a minus four next to *Sarah Simpson*? She couldn't stand it.

Sarah took her blue pencil to the front of the room and sharpened it. She walked back and forth behind the teacher's chair, trying to see over her shoulder. *Tinka, tinka, tinka,* went the bells pinned to the bottom of her yellow top.

Mrs. Gold was resting one hand on the grade book right where Sarah wanted to see. Sarah went back to her seat and got her green pencil. She took that to the front of the room to sharpen. *Tinka, tinka, tinka,* went the bells.

She leaned over her teacher's shoulder to look at the grade book. Then she leaned over a little more.

Plunk. The pencil slipped out of Sarah's hand and landed on the teacher's desk.

Mrs. Gold turned around. "Do you want something, Sarah?" she asked.

"She wants to be Emily Watson," somebody said.

Sarah glared at the girl who said it. "No, I don't," she said. And then she said to the teacher, "I just wanted to be sure Miss Bowers wrote down the right grade for spelling."

Mrs. Gold checked the book. "You got them all right," she said. "Very good, Sarah. But I'm afraid you're going to have to take off those bells. Save them for a holiday party, okay?"

Some of the kids laughed as Sarah went out in the hall to the restroom.

Stupid bells! she thought, as she took off her top and unpinned the bells around the bottom. *Stupid idea!* Her ideas were getting dumber all the time!

It didn't matter what her name was. It didn't matter what she wore. Wearing bells and putting a *T* in your name didn't make you special. Anyone could wear bells. Anyone could have a *T*. Anyone would know you were coming if you put bells on the bottoms of your clothes.

She felt yucky at recess. But when she saw Tim Wong sitting on one of the swings without swinging, he didn't look so happy, either. He was digging the toe of his sneaker in the dirt as the swing twisted slowly from side to side.

Sarah walked over and sat in the swing next to him.

"Hey," she said.

"Hey," said Tim.

Sarah studied him for a moment. "I heard that your dad might close your restaurant. That's not true, is it?" she asked.

Tim shrugged. "I don't know," he said. "But if he does, we'll have to move."

"Wongs' has the best chicken wings in the whole city," Sarah said.

"I know. It's my grandfather's recipe," Tim told her. "But we don't have enough customers."

"Well, when we come on Saturday there will be five of us. Peter and his grandmother are coming, too," said Sarah.

"I'll tell my dad," said Tim.

If anyone needed bells to cheer him up, it was Tim Wong, Sarah thought. *But bells probably wouldn't make him feel better, either.*

Seven

Anyone Can Eat Squid!

On Saturday evening, Sarah and her mom and Riley stopped by Peter's apartment. Peter and his grandmother came out, and together they walked the four blocks to Wongs' Restaurant.

There were two red dragon statues out front. The door had a round look, which gave Sarah the feeling that she was stepping through a circle.

Inside, the wind chimes tinkled gently from the ceiling, and a huge fish tank bubbled softly to one side.

"Oh, my!" said Granny Belle, smiling and looking around her. "I'm so glad I wore my Sunday hat."

Sarah and Riley and Peter went over to the fish tank while they waited for their table to be ready.

"If you were a fish, which one would you be?" Peter asked. "I'd be the blue one with the yellow stripes."

"I'd be the big orange one!" said Riley, pointing.

But Sarah kept watching till she found the most extraordinary fish of all. "I'd be the black-and-white one, with red on its tail," she said.

A waiter in a red jacket motioned to them. "Please follow me," he said and led them to a table in the center of the room.

Tim was there waiting for them. "Hi, Peter. Hi, Sarah," he said.

"This is Tim from school," Peter told his grandmother. "His dad owns this restaurant." And to Tim, he said, "This is my grandmother, Granny Belle."

Granny Belle studied the boy with the shiny black hair. "If your dad owns this restaurant, why aren't you fat?" she asked, giving his cheek a little pinch. "I would think you'd be eating all the time."

Tim looked surprised. Peter looked embarrassed, but the others laughed, so Tim laughed, too.

"I'm too busy to eat all the time," he said.

There were several families eating nearby. The family at the large round table by the window seemed to be celebrating a birthday, and Tim said that this table, with the red cloth, was saved for special occasions.

Sarah liked eating at Wongs'. It was a warm place, a noisy place, a friendly place to have dinner, even though half the tables were empty.

Tim left and came back with a booster seat for Riley.

"No!" said Riley. "No booster seat!"

He climbed up on his chair and sat down, but the table was as high as his chin.

"Riley, you can hardly see over the table!" said his mother.

"No booster seat!" Riley said. "Boosters are for babies."

Tim went away. Riley tried to reach his glass of water, but he was too low. Tim came back again. This time he had the Yellow Pages.

"How about a phone book?" he asked Riley.

Riley looked at Tim. He looked at the Yellow Pages. "Okay," he said. He got up and let Tim slide the phone book beneath him. Everyone was happy.

The waiter in the red jacket passed menus around the table. He missed Riley.

"I want one!" said Riley.

"Honey, you can't read," said Mom. "Here. You can share mine."

"I want one of my own!" said Riley loudly.

"I'm afraid someone could have used a nap today," Mom told Granny Belle.

"I don't take naps!" yelled Riley.

Tim hurried back to the table. He gave Riley a menu. Riley opened it up and pretended to read. The menu was upside down.

"What would you like, Mrs. Grant?" asked Mom.

Granny Belle studied the menu. "I would like Wongs' Wings and a plate of Chinese vegetables," she said.

"I think we'll order a big platter of Wongs' Wings, and we'll all share," said Mom. "Also some beef and green peppers."

"I want Wongs' Wings and ice cream," said Riley.

"I want wings and wonton soup," said Peter.

But Sarah wanted to be different. She wanted to try something she had never had before.

"I'll take the squid," she told the waiter.

After the man in the red jacket had taken their order to the kitchen, Peter said to Sarah, "Do you know what squid is?"

"Fish?" said Sarah.

"Sort of like octopus," said Peter.

Riley's eyes grew wide. "She's going to

51

eat a big old octopus?" he cried.

Peter laughed. "Well, *some* squid are forty feet long!" he said.

Sarah's stomach felt queasy. She imagined six waiters coming to the table carrying a forty-foot-long squid. But she wouldn't back out now. If people could eat snails in France, she could eat squid here in Chicago.

The waiter brought a teapot. Granny Belle, in her Sunday hat, filled the little cups and passed them around.

Tim Wong came bringing chopsticks and showed Riley how to hold them.

The barbecued chicken wings arrived, and they were delicious.

The Chinese vegetables and rice were delivered to Granny Belle, and she said they were wonderful, just like vegetables grown in the country.

And then the waiter brought the squid. Sarah was glad that it was cut up into little pieces and she did not have to eat a whole one.

Everyone watched as she put some on her plate. Everyone watched as she picked up a piece on her fork.

I will not throw up. I will not throw up, Sarah told herself. Into her mouth it went.

Sarah stared down at her lap as she chewed. It tasted a little like chicken. It tasted a little like fish. It tasted a lot like rubber bands and was a little slippery going down, but she swallowed.

Everyone at the table clapped, and Sarah was embarrassed. People at the other tables turned to see what the clapping was all about, as though she had done something special.

Right, thought Sarah. *Anyone could eat squid.*

Eight

Sarah's Fortune

The food went around and around the table—the chicken wings, the vegetables, the beef with green peppers, even the squid.

Tim Wong was busy helping out the waiters wherever he could.

"How did you like the squid?" he asked Sarah, as he helped remove their plates.

"It was different," she said.

"How about dessert?" asked Mom.

Sarah, Peter, and Riley all wanted ice cream. While they were waiting for it, Tim brought his father and grandfather over to the table.

"So glad to have you," Tim's father said, as he and Mom shook hands. Mom introduced Granny Belle and said, "We love your restaurant. We're hoping you will stay in business a long, long time."

Mr. Wong spoke to the old grandfather in Chinese. The grandfather stopped smiling and answered in Chinese. Mr. Wong repeated what the old man had said: "He says it would be a sad day if Wongs' had to close, but we need more customers to keep it open."

"But your food is wonderful!" said Mom. "Everyone loves Wongs' Wings. They're the best in Chicago."

Mr. Wong repeated it to the grandfather in Chinese, and the grandfather answered again: "Ah, but does the rest of Chicago even know we are here? It's too bad the restaurant isn't on a busier street, but we cannot afford it."

"Well, we wish you much luck," Mom said. "And dinner tonight was delicious."

The dessert came then, and everyone got a fortune cookie.

Granny Belle, being the oldest, broke open her cookie first and took out the small slip of paper. She tipped back her head to see better through her glasses.

"*New friends will seek you out*," she read.

"Well, we're not exactly *new* friends, but I hope that many more people in our apartment building will want to be friends with you and Peter," said Mom.

She opened her cookie next and read her fortune: "*Time is more precious than silver*," she read. "But I knew that already."

"My turn!" said Riley. He pulled out his slip of paper and pretended to read it to himself. The others tried not to laugh.

"What does it say?" asked Sarah.

Riley pressed it against his shirt and wouldn't say.

"Can I see it?" said Sarah.

"No!" said Riley.

"Could *I* read it then?" asked Peter.

Riley gave the slip of paper to Peter. "*A little mouth makes much noise*," Peter read, and everyone burst into laughter.

"I wonder if Tim had anything to do with these fortunes," Mom joked. "What does your fortune say, Peter?"

Peter read, "*Youth is restless; age is wise.*"

Granny Belle nodded her head. "And see that you remember that, Peter. Your old granny knows what she's talking about."

Sarah was the last one to open her fortune cookie. She hoped it would tell her about her future. "*Every good deed starts with a good idea*," she read. That wasn't a fortune! Sarah was disappointed, but she didn't complain.

"Well, are we ready to go?" asked Mom

finally. "It's been a fun evening."

"It has indeed," said Granny Belle. "And thank you for inviting us."

As they stood up to leave, Sarah saw that the restaurant was still half empty. Tim's father and grandfather were having a serious talk at a table in the corner. The grandfather pointed at the empty tables and chairs and shook his head.

"Good-bye, everyone," Tim said, as Sarah and the others stepped back out the round door and walked down the sidewalk, past the two red dragons. Riley tried to hide the chopsticks he was taking with him, but Tim laughed and told him they were his to keep.

It was a lovely night, and there was a breeze from the lake. Riley jabbered all the way home, making his fortune seem all the more true. But Sarah was thinking about Wongs' Restaurant and the sad look on Tim's face that day on the swings. She wished she had a good idea. A big idea. Any idea at all, in fact, of how to help out.

Nine

Wongs' Wings

Sarah lay in bed and listened to the night noises of the city. Her bed was on one side of a window, and Riley's was on the other. She could hear taxicabs honking, tires squealing, sirens going, bells tolling—sometimes all at the same time.

When Mom came by to say good night, Sarah said, "If not enough people know about Wongs' Restaurant, why doesn't Mr. Wong put an ad in the paper?"

"Because that costs too much money, Sarah," her mom said, pulling the curtain.

"Why doesn't he tell about it on TV?" asked Riley.

"That costs even more," Mom told him.

Sarah listened to the bathwater running as her mother got ready for bed. *To get customers, a restaurant should advertise*, Sarah thought. But to get enough money to advertise, a restaurant needed more customers. It seemed like a problem without an answer.

Maybe the next day she would make some signs herself, she decided. She would print *EAT AT WONGS'* in big red letters on notebook paper. Then she'd tape the signs to the telephone poles on their block.

In the morning Sarah got up before anyone else and put on her clothes. She got out her notebook paper and a red felt-tip pen. After she had made the signs, she took them outside and taped them to four telephone poles. But later, halfway through her cereal, it started to rain.

Sarah went to the window and stared down at the street. The raindrops on the window glass looked like tears.

It rained harder and harder. Riley slept on and on. Her mom slept on and on. Sarah had hoped she could tell her dad about the signs. He called them every Sunday evening from overseas. But now her signs were ruined, and there would be nothing to tell.

When the rain stopped for a short while, Sarah went back outside. One of her signs had blown away. One had ripped apart. The red ink on the other two had dripped and smeared so that Sarah could hardly read the words.

Stupid, stupid, stupid! she thought, as she tore them all down. *EAT AT WONGS'* didn't tell anyone anything. It didn't even tell where the restaurant was.

She went back inside the apartment building and started up the stairs. She hoped no one would see her, but Peter was standing outside his door in his outer-space pajamas, picking up the Sunday newspaper.

"Want to read the comics after I've finished?" he asked.

"No. We already get a newspaper," Sarah said, and tried to walk on by.

"Your arm's bleeding," said Peter.

Sarah looked down. The red ink from her signs had come off on her arm and hand.

"Stupid signs! Stupid idea!" Sarah muttered. "I just wanted to help the Wongs, and it was all wrong. Every idea I get turns out stupid!"

Sarah sat down on the stairs and told him what she had been trying to do.

Peter looked at one of the signs. "It wasn't such a bad idea," he said. "It sounds sort of like scolding, though."

"What do you mean?" asked Sarah.

"*EAT AT WONGS'* is too much like *BRUSH YOUR TEETH. GO TO BED!*" said Peter.

"Yeah, it stinks." Sarah sniffled a little and tried not to cry. She sat with her chin in her hands. "Signs shouldn't be on telephone poles, anyway. They should be on the backs of buses. They should be moving all around the city so a lot of people can see them. In fact, they should be on the backs of *people!*"

Suddenly her eyes grew wider. Her mouth fell open.

"T-shirts!" she said. "We could put the message on T-shirts and wear them all around the neighborhood."

"Who's going to paint it on?" Peter asked.

"Guess!" said Sarah. She jumped up and raced upstairs.

Mom was in her robe making coffee. "I wondered where you were," she said. "Then I heard you talking with Peter on the stairs. What a gray sky! But *you* look cheerful for a rainy morning, Sarah."

"I have an idea to help the Wongs!" Sarah said excitedly. "We could put an ad for their restaurant on the back of a T-shirt, and I could wear it around the neighborhood. Maybe Peter could wear one, too."

"And me!" said Riley, coming to the table, rubbing his eyes.

"Could you paint them for us, Mom?" Sarah asked.

Her mother looked thoughtful. "What would you like me to paint?"

"Something that would make people want to eat there," Sarah said.

Her mother poured cereal into Riley's bowl, then milk. "Well," she said, "what's the first thing you think of when you hear the word *Wongs'*?"

"Wongs' Wings—the barbecued chicken," said Sarah.

"And what is the first thing you *see* when you think of Wongs'?" asked her mother.

Sarah closed her eyes for a second. "The red dragons," she said.

"Perfect!" said Mom. "I was thinking of the tropical-fish tank, but a dragon is even better. Why don't I paint a red dragon for the front of the T-shirt, and on the back we can print *Wongs' Wings* with their phone number."

Sarah rushed to hug her mother and almost tumbled into her lap.

"Can I have one, too?" said Riley, wiping milk off his mouth.

"I'll tell you what," said Mom. "I'll paint it so we can transfer the design to any T-shirt."

And before she had even finished her coffee, she sat down at her drawing board under the skylight and began to sketch the dragon.

Ten

Here Comes Sarah Simpson!

All morning the rain came down, and all morning Sarah sat beside her mother, watching her draw the dragon. Mom had twisted its body around so that its head was facing its tail. There was smoke coming out of its nostrils and fire coming out of its mouth.

Riley played with his Matchbox cars over on the windowsill. Sometimes he wandered over to watch, too.

Sarah got up once to make peanut-butter sandwiches for all of them. She got up again to read a book to Riley and help him work a puzzle.

But when it came time to paint the sketch of the dragon, both Sarah and Riley wanted to watch.

"What color should we make the eyes?" asked Mom.

"Yellow," said Sarah, "with big black dots in the middle."

Her mother carefully dabbed yellow paint for the eyes.

"Wings?" asked Mom.

"Yes! To go with *Wongs' Wings*," said Sarah.

"Good thinking," said Mom. "Claws?"

"Yes! Make that dragon have big old claws," said Riley.

One o'clock became two. Two o'clock became three, and Mom was still painting. She did not even want to eat. She just wanted to finish the dragon.

"It's scary looking!" Riley said in a whisper, as though the creature might rise up from the paper and bite him.

Mom put down her brush at last. She sat back and looked at her dragon. "This is the finest dragon I have ever painted," she said softly. "I really love it! I love the way the light shines on its scaly back."

"I do, too!" said Sarah. "See, Mom? You *are* the best at something!"

"But it was your idea, Sarah. There wouldn't be any dragon at all—any T-shirts at all—if it wasn't for you. *Every good deed starts with a good idea*, remember."

The phone rang. It was Sarah's father.

"Hi, Dad!" Sarah cried, when she answered. And before she handed the phone to her mother and Riley, she told her father all about Wongs' Restaurant and the dragon Mom had made.

"That's my Sarah!" said Dad. "The Idea Girl!"

When the Idea Girl got home from school the next day, there were four T-shirts—one for her, one for Riley, one for Peter, and one for Tim Wong. Each had a wonderful red dragon on the front. On the back, in letters that looked a little Chinese, it said *Wongs' Wings*, and beneath that was a phone number.

"Oh, Mom, they're great!" said Sarah.

"Put one on," said Mom.

Riley put on his, too, and together he and Sarah went down to the third floor to give one to Peter.

"Now if that isn't something!" said Granny

Belle, as Peter pranced about the apartment in his dragon T-shirt. He wiggled his body back and forth so it looked as if the dragon was moving. He jerked the bottom of his T-shirt from left to right and made it look as though the dragon was swishing its tail. He sucked in his chest, then thrust it forward again to make it look as though the dragon was breathing in and out.

Sarah and Riley laughed at Peter, and so did Granny Belle. "Peter Jefferson Grant, I think you're giving that dragon a bellyache," she said.

The next day, Sarah and Peter wore their T-shirts to school. Everyone wanted to touch the dragon. All the kids wished they had a red dragon T-shirt, too. Even Mrs. Gold wanted to have one.

But Tim Wong was happiest of all. And when school was out that day and Sarah got home, Mr. Wong called and wanted to speak with Mom. After she had finished talking to him, Mom hung up and turned to Sarah.

"Guess what?" she said. "Mr. Wong is so pleased with Tim's T-shirt, that he wants to buy the design. He wants to put it on T-shirts to sell at the restaurant."

"Will you sell it to him?" asked Sarah.

"No. I'll *give* it to him," said her mother. "It will be our gift, Sarah, yours and mine, to keep our favorite restaurant open."

Every day, more and more kids showed up at school wearing the red dragon T-shirt. Emily Watson had one and so did David Bork. Almost every day, it seemed, when Sarah and Peter walked home from school, someone stopped them to ask, "Where did you get those wonderful T-shirts? I'd like to get one for myself."

Granny Belle decided she needed one to wear to the grocery store. Mom got one to wear to the library. It was hard to walk around the neighborhood without seeing at least one other person wearing a white T-shirt with a red dragon on the front.

Sarah wore hers to school. She wore it to church. She wore it to the playground, to her music lesson, and her book club.

And finally, one day at school Tim told her, "We're going to keep Wongs' open! We're so busy, we had to hire one of my cousins to help out. We're so busy, we had to buy two more tables. We want you to come to dinner again, as guests of my father and grandfather."

Sarah was so happy, she wanted to turn cartwheels. She was so excited, she wanted to yell. This was the biggest, the best, the greatest, the most splendiferous idea she had ever had in her entire life.

She had not bought it in a store. She had not gotten it from a drawer. She had hatched it right up there in her head. Sarah could hardly wait to get home that afternoon and tell her mom.

On Saturday evening Sarah's family went back to Wongs'. Almost all the tables were full. Tim was busy, Mr. Wong was busy, all the waiters were hurrying back and forth, and the old grandfather was sitting at a corner table quickly folding napkins.

When Tim saw Sarah there in the doorway, he said, "Here comes Sarah Simpson!"

She looked like any other girl in a red dragon T-shirt, but Tim led Sarah and her mother and Riley over to the big round table by the window, where a sign beside the teapot read *Reserved*. It was the table with the red cloth, the table for celebrations. And tonight it was the table for someone special.